Stories for 4 year-olds

BONNEY
PRESS

Contents

Welcome to Stories for 4-year-olds 3

It Takes Two to T'wit T'woo 5

Chomp 35

I'm Not Scared 65

Jack, Be Nimble 95

Mary, Mary, Quite Contrary......................... 96

Published by Bonney Press
an imprint of Hinkler Books Pty Ltd
45–55 Fairchild Street
Heatherton Victoria 3202 Australia
www.hinkler.com

BONNEY PRESS

© Hinkler Books Pty Ltd 2019

Authors: Paula Knight, Melissa Mattox, Dan Crisp
Illustrators: Guiliano Ferri, Mark Chambers, Lee Wildish, Jon Contino, Lauren Hom
Editorial: Zoe Antony
Design: Aimee Forde
Prepress: Splitting Image

ISBN: 978 1 4889 1441 6

Printed and bound in China

Welcome to
Stories for 4-year-olds

Storytime can be the snuggliest part of the day
with your lively 4-year-old—and a good storybook can ignite your child's
imagination and teach them lots about the world, and themselves!

Reading together is also one of the best things you can do for your child's
development. At four, your once tiny baby is unmistakably a big boy or
girl! And with a longer attention span and the ability to hold complex
conversations, more than ever this is the time that reading together
is vital! Getting your child excited about books can do wonders to
smooth their transition to school, and promote a lifetime of independent
reading and learning.

Stories for 4-year-olds contains three fantastic stories to enjoy
with your young dynamo, specially chosen to be absorbing and entertaining
for 4-year-old kids. We've also included two fun nursery rhymes to finish
with a flourish!

Follow Olive Owl in the
gorgeously illustrated *It Takes Two to T'wit
T'woo*, as she searches for a singing buddy and
meets many animal friends along the way.

Then get ready for school with *Chomp*—a heart-warming story
about a young shark who struggles to fit in on his first day of school.
Your child will love the colorful undersea illustrations and uplifting
message about not giving up!

Finally, meet the bravest cat ever in *I'm Not Scared*. They're not afraid of
ghosts, ghouls or grizzly bears—they're not a scaredy-cat! But who's that
knocking at their door? The hilarious tale pokes riotous fun
at all the fantastic creatures you can think of.

Happy reading!

It Takes Two to T'wit T'woo

Paula Knight • Guiliano Ferri

Olive Owl could only say "t'wit."

"T'wit, t'wit," she went. She couldn't say "t'woo."

She dearly wished to meet another owl who could hoot "t'woo," so that they could "t'wit t'woo" together.

Olive perched high up in her tree and called out,
"T'wit... T'wit..."

She listened carefully with her pointy ears.

"Ribbit... Ribbit..." came the reply.

"Who's there?" said Olive.

"I don't suppose 'ribbit' will do?" asked the frog.

"No, 'ribbit' will never do," said Olive.

She really needed a "t'woo" to go with her "t'wit."

"T'wit... T'wit... T'wit..." called Olive, trying again.

Her pointy ears were pricked, listening carefully.

"Quack, quack! Quack, quack!" came the reply.

"Who's there?" said Olive.

"I don't suppose a 'quack' will do?" asked the duck.

"I'm sorry," said Olive, sadly. She was hoping for a "t'woo."

This time, Olive shouted, **"T'wit!"** a bit louder, hoping that somewhere, someone with a lovely "t'woo" might hear her.

"GRRRRRRRRRR," came the reply.

"Who's there?" called Olive.

"I don't suppose a 'grrrrrr' will do?" asked the great big grizzly bear.

Olive sighed, "No, not at all, I'm afraid."

What she really wanted was a hooty tooty "t'woo!"

"T'wit... T'wit... T'wit, t'wit, t'wit, t'wit, t'wit!"

This time, Olive carried on "t'witting" over and over again, hoping that her dream owl would surely hear her.

"Anyone there?" she called out.

Before long, new friends surrounded Olive. Everyone had heard her "t'wits," and had come to find out what all the fuss was about. Everyone, that was, apart from Albert.

Hee-haw

Oink

Meow

Buzzz

Squeak

Hisss

Woof

17

Albert lived far away, in another tree, in another wood, over the hill.

"T'WOO," he tooted. But nobody could hear him. What Albert wanted more than ever, was a "t'wit" to go with his "t'woo."

Somewhere in the distance, he thought he could hear a terrible din of quacking, oinking, growling, croaking, hissing, meowing, buzzing, squeaking, and woofing. And the odd hee-haw...

Hee-haw
Meow
Squeak   Quack
Oink
Croak
Buzz
Growl
Woof
Hisss

Olive looked down at the duck, the cat, the donkey,
the frog, the dog, the snake, the bee, the pig, the mouse,
and the great big grizzly bear.

"What will you do if you can't find a 't'woo?'"
they asked.

"I don't know. Please can you help me?" said Olive.

Together, they all took a huge deep breath...

"T'wi-i-i-t!"

they shouted at the
tops of their voices.

They hushed and listened for a reply. Sure enough, from a far-away wood over the hill, someone had heard them…

"T'woo... T'woo-hoo!" hooted Albert, hardly able to believe what he was hearing.

"T'wi-i-i-t!"

There it was again!

Albert was excited and set off in the direction of the "t'wit," calling, **"T'wooo!"** as he flew.

"**Woohoo!** I heard it, I really heard it!" said Olive, her feathers all a-fluster.

Albert landed on the tree, right next to her.
They had found each other at last.

"T'WOO!" he said.

"T'WIT!" said Olive.

"GRRRRR," said the great big grizzly bear.
"That's the wrong way round!"

"T'wit... T'woo!" said Olive and Albert, one after the other.

The animals cheered. Olive and Albert continued "t'witting" and "t'wooing" together until dawn, when they snuggled up for a well-earned sleep.

Many people hear "t'wit, t'woo" and don't realize that it takes two owls to make the sound: the female calls "t'wit" and the male answers with "t'woo."

Tawny owls build their nests in holes in trees. They can only see as well as we do at night, but they use their extra sensitive ears to hunt for food.

Once a couple, tawny owls usually stay together for life.

To my son Eric

Chomp

Written by Melissa Mattox
Illustrated by Mark Chambers

Today was Chomp's first day at school. He was afraid he wouldn't make any new friends. He swam slowly behind his dad towards the coral gates of the school as the other fish darted and splashed out of their way.

"Keep your dorsal fin up and don't forget to smile," said Chomp's dad reassuringly.

Chomp nodded, but he could hear whispers from a passing pod of dolphins. "I hope I'm not in the shark's class," said one.

"There's no way anyone is going to want to sit next to him," hissed another.

Chomp tried to remember what his dad said about smiling, but he knew it wouldn't be easy.

It seemed that everyone already had lots of friends.

Chomp tried to introduce himself to his fellow classmates. He remembered what his father said and did his best smile.

"Hello, I'm..."

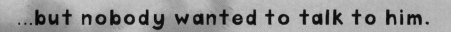
...but nobody wanted to talk to him.

At the playground, things didn't get much better.

Chomp tried to join in
with hide-and-seek.

"...nine, ten.
I'm coming
to get you!"

...but nobody wanted to play.

Everywhere he went, Chomp felt like he didn't belong.

When lunchtime came, Chomp still hadn't made one single friend.

He collected his lunch but noticed something was missing. He swam over to a nearby table.

"**AHHHH!** Please don't eat us!" screamed the crab.

AHHHH!

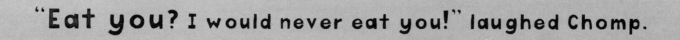
"Eat you? I would never eat you!" laughed Chomp.

"I'm a vegetarian! Could you possibly pass the sea salt please?"

After that, the other fish found they had a lot more in common with Chomp than they'd thought.

From then on, things seemed to go much easier!

Chomp and his class went to visit historical sites.

They practiced their
fishing-line knots.

And they even played Chomp's favorite game of chase!

By the end of the day, Chomp had made so many friends that by the time his dad showed up, he didn't want to leave.

"Please, can I stay here?" he begged. Chomp's dad laughed.

"Don't worry," said Miss Blowfish. "Tomorrow's lesson is something you can really sink your teeth into."

I'm NOT SCARED

Dan Crisp   Lee Wildish

I'm not scared of MONSTERS. They don't frighten me.

Even ones with **scary eyes**;

I'd have them round for tea!

I'm not scared of GIANTS,

hanging out in the wild.

Even if they're man-eating beasts, and I am just a child.

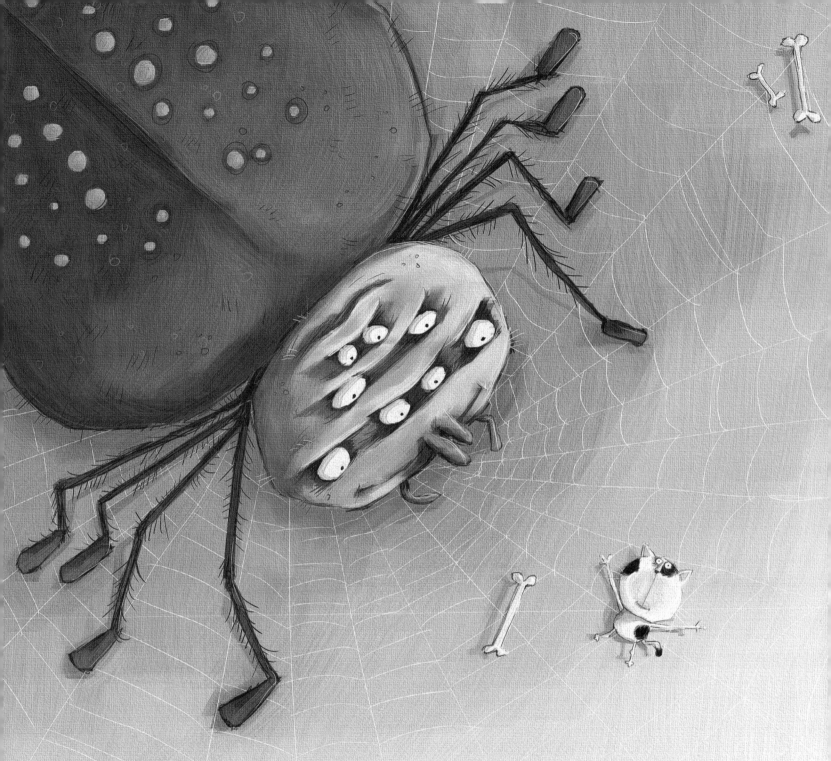

I'm not scared of SPIDERS,

be they as big as a bus.

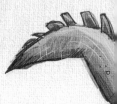

Cornered by a crowd of
CROCS;

I wouldn't make a fuss.

I'm even fine with WITCHES, as evil as they can be.
GHOSTS, GHOULS and VAMPIRES—

they don't frighten me!

I'm not scared of **SKELETONS**,

rattling all their bones.

Or strange sounds from the cellar;
the creepy moans and groans.

I'm not scared of OGRES and their great big beady eyes.

Lurking under bridges; they can't make me cry.

The
lions

and the
tigers,

great **grizzly bears** too.

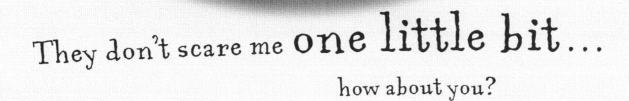

They don't scare me **one little bit...**

how about you?

I'm not scared of JELLYFISH,

SHARKS or

WRIGGLING EELS.

I turn my back and swim away,

kicking with my heels.

I'm not afraid of **DRAGONS**,

with their fire and scaly skin.

ROARING, *SCREAMING* and jumping about—

all I do is grin.

I might be scared of DINOSAURS,

if they were still around.

Hang on there just a minute.

What's that
funny sound?

You'll have to please excuse me;
there's someone at the door . . .

Jack, Be Nimble

JACK, BE NIMBLE,
JACK, BE QUICK,
JACK, JUMP OVER
The CANDLESTICK!

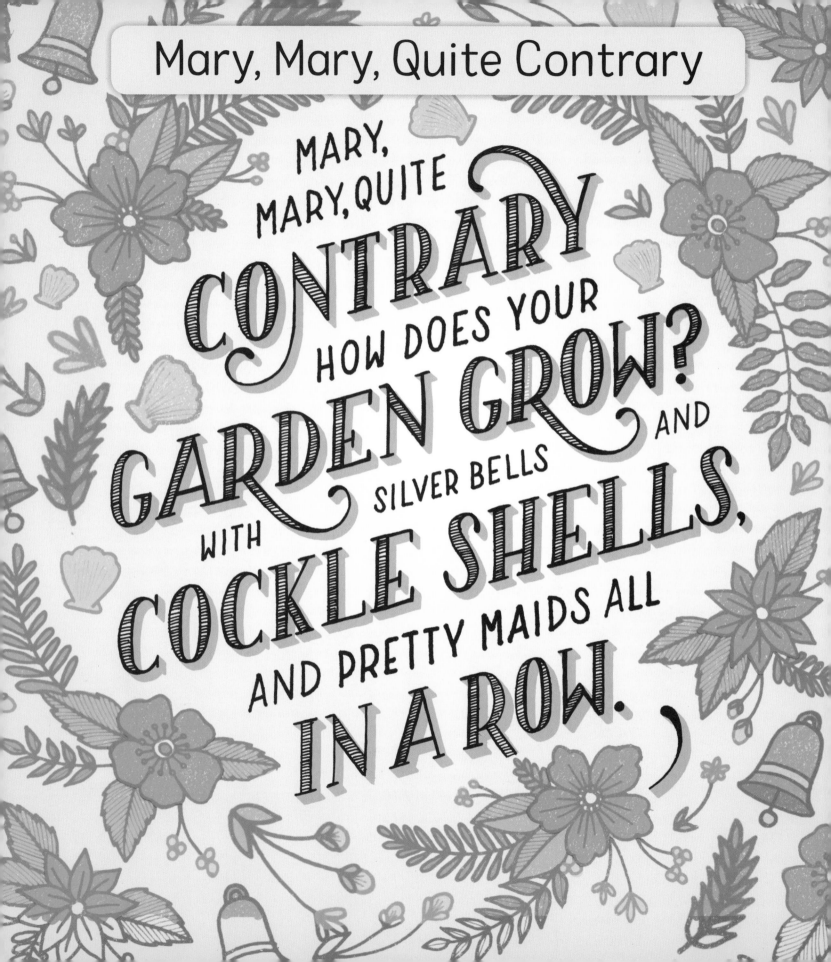